Hello, Mars!

Special thanks to William I. Purdy, Jr.,
former Director of the Mars Observer
Project, Jet Propulsion Laboratory,
Pasadena, California, for his valuable
time and technical assistance.

10 9 8 7 6 5 4 3 2 1

Library of Congress Cataloging-in-Publication Data

Williams, Geoffrey T.
  Hello, Mars!/ by Geoffrey T. Williams: illustrated by Yvonne
Cherbak.
  p.   cm.
  Summary: A boy travels from Earth to Mars to join his parents, part
of the first group of colonists to Mars. A cassette accompanies the
book.
  [1. Interplanetary voyages—Fiction. 2. Science fiction.]
I. Cherbak, Yvonne, ill.   II. Title.
PZ7.W65915He 1989
[Fic]—dc19   89-3798
                                                          CIP
                                                          AC

  ISBN: 0-8431-2733-3: hardcover book

  ISBN 0-8431-2745-7: hardcover book & cassette

Hello, Mars!

by Geoffrey T. Williams
Illustrated by Yvonne Cherbak

PRICE STERN SLOAN

Los Angeles

SPACE MAIL TRANSMISSION AUGUST 12, 2071.
FROM: A.C. Jones, drop-box 12-B, Bradbury, Mars.
TO: Bellavia M. Charming-Jones, 94582-A, Sub-level 18, Phoenix/Tucson
Metroplex, United North America, Earth. Recording.

"Grandma. Sorry I haven't written for a while. Let's see, I've been here . . . has it been three months already? School's the same as on Earth, except for Survival Training—and the fact that there are only twelve kids on the whole planet. This is the first weekend Dad's let me take the six-wheeler out . . ."

"Hey, Arky! Look at this!"

" . . . of course, I'm not alone. That's Ilena on the radio. She came with me today. Just a sec, Grandma, I better remind her . . . hey! Wait up! Don't get too close! That edge could crumble!"

"Come on."

"In a minute. There's no air, no water, and nothing will grow outside the biosphere domes and the hydroponic gardens. You can't survive outside without a pressure suit, but the six-wheeler always has emergency sup-plies. It's not really dangerous. You just have to be careful. I never thought I'd want to live anywhere except Earth. But there's something about Mars . . . it's hard to describe . . . remember when we talked about pio-neers? And living on the edge of the frontier? Well, here I am, on a cliff above Candor Chasma, a deep canyon that's part of Valles Marinaris— Mariner Valley—named after the first satellite to send back pictures of Mars in 1965, over one hundred years ago. You know how the Grand Canyon looks? Well, Valles Marinaris is three times deeper and ten times longer. The rocks are red and orange and rugged. It must be two, three kliks (that's kilometers) down to the old lakebed . . ."

"This is a Satellite Early Warning Weather Alert. Stand by for emergency weather information on all frequencies . . . "

"Great! Now what? I'd better finish this letter later, Grandma."

"Dust storm detected minus twenty degrees south, seventy degrees west, heading northwest at 100 kliks-per-hour. Expected to hit Bradbury in approximately eight hours. Emergency precautions recommended."

"Ilena? Are you monitoring?"

"I heard it."

"Then come on. We have to head back."

"Darn! I'll be right—Ohhhh! Arky! I'm falling! Help! Arkeeeeeeee!"

"What, what? Oh, no! . . . Ilena?"

The ancient Martian rock was cracked and crumbled where she had fallen. Luckily, she had landed on a narrow ledge several hundred meters down the side. But she wasn't moving. "Lena, I see you now. Is your pressure suit okay? What? Your radio's breaking up. I can't hear you. Can you hear me? Good. No! Don't try to move! That ledge might give. I'm going to radio for help and get some more rope. Don't worry, I'll be right back!"

"Repeating. Dust storm detected. Emergency precautions recommended."

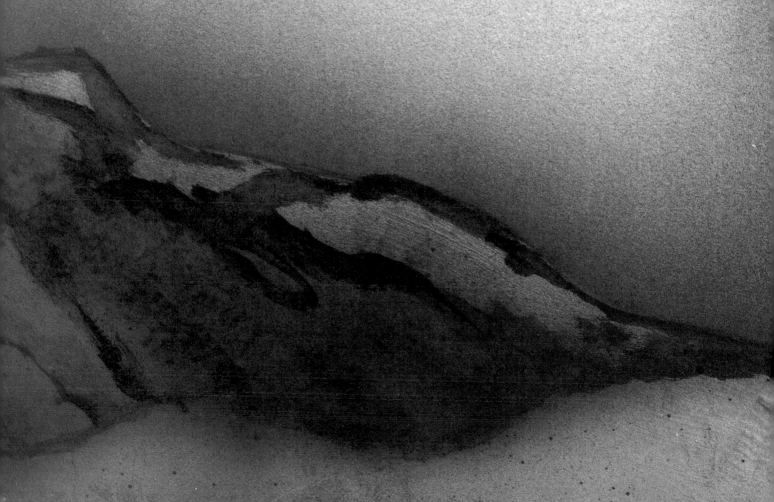

Thanks to Mars's lighter gravity and my Earth muscles, I was able to move in short jumps, a couple of meters at a time. But the pressure suit was awkward and it seemed to take forever to get to the six-wheeler. I started it up, drove to within a few meters of the edge, and got out. "Where's the rope? Come on, Jones! Where is it? Faster, Jones. Faster. Come on . . . ah! Found it!" It seemed the faster I tried to move, the clumsier I got. When I realized I was talking to myself to keep from thinking about the danger, I took a few deep breaths and slowed down. "No time for panic, Jones. Take it easy . . . "

I tied the rope first around myself and then the six-wheeler. "I'm on my way, Lena." I took another deep breath and lowered myself over the cliff. I could feel the gravel slipping under my heavy boots.

My hands and arms grew tired after a few minutes. My shoulders ached. The rope seemed to want to slip through my gloves. I made the mistake of relaxing for a second and almost lost it completely. I slid and scrambled and clawed, looking for any kind of a ledge or crevice. Finally I found a toehold and came to a stop. Taking an extra turn of rope around my hands, I rested, breathing heavily. Below me, Ilena lay unmoving. Going down was the easy part . . .

How did I ever get myself into this mess? Oh yeah, I remember . . .

HAPPY BIRTHDAY

"Good morning, Arky. It's six-forty-five, October 4, 2070. You now have thirty seconds to disable."

"Mmurff?"

"You now have fifteen seconds to disable."

"What . . . whdimzt?"

"You now have ten seconds to disable."

"Okay, okay. I'm getting . . . "

"Three. Two. One."

"Wait! No!" I lunged for the alarm clock. Too late. The noise that came from the speakers was deafening: screaming jets, roaring trains, trumpeting elephants. By the time it stopped I was wide awake.

"And . . . Happy Birthday!"

"I think it's time I re-programmed you."

"That's option 'R' on the main console . . . "

I punched the silence button and went in to take a shower.

October 4th might not mean much to some people, but if you took Space History you might remember that October 4, 1957, was the day a country called the Soviet Union launched Sputnik—the first satellite to orbit Earth. It's no big deal now. If ISSA—that's the Inner System Space Agency—has to put up a satellite, they pack it in a scramjet cargo hold along with the tourist baggage, then turn it over to a launch team after docking at the space station. The launch team just pushes it out the door into space. Well, it's almost that simple. Anyway, Sputnik and I share the same, uh, launch date: I was born on October 4th too—in 2057, that is—exactly a century after Sputnik. And today was my thirteenth birthday. I didn't know it at the time, but I was about to write my own page in space history.

The intercom clicked on. "Happy Birthday, Arky!"

"Thanks, Grandma."

"There's a call for you."

"Voice or visual? I'm not done dressing."

"It's holophone. I think it's your mom and dad."

"What?!" I couldn't imagine my folks calling "holo." There's an old joke about phone rates being astronomical—only nobody laughs. A holographic call from Mom and Dad would cost over one thousand dollars. You see, they were on Mars.

The laser beams hummed as they formed the realistic, three-dimensional image in front of me. "Hi, sweetheart. Happy Birthday!"

"Mom! It *is* you! Oh, gee, that's stupid." I was so excited I almost forgot—Mars was ninety-six million kliks from Earth. So, since we still hadn't figured out a way to beat the speed of light, it wasn't a live call. There would be a five-minute delay before they could hear me, and another five minutes before I could hear their answer.

"We can't talk long. TRI-EMCO authorized our bonus and we just bought your ticket! I'll let your dad give you the details."

The house Comm-center must have taped their call the night before, probably relayed through LEO-3 Commport—the giant low Earth orbit Communications Space Station built and operated by Inter Planetary Telephone & Telegraph (no, I don't know what a telegraph is, either). Messages from all over the inner solar system—Farside and Tycho City on the Moon, or any of TRI-EMCO's Martian bases like P3 on Phobos and their asteroid mining outposts—are received at LEO-3 and relayed to Earth. Mom and Dad worked at Bradbury, the big mining center on the surface of Mars.

"Arky! Happy Birthday! We sure have missed you! I'll bet you thought this day would never come! Some birthday present, huh? Your ticket's at Mojave Interplanetary Spaceport. The launch window opens next week. Scramjet to LEO-4 and transfer to L-1, then to the ISS CLARKE. You should make Marsfall in a few months. Hey, wait'll you hit a baseball at one-third gravity! Here's your mom again."

"Bradbury is so exciting, Arky. And Olympus is just a few hours away. There's so much to see. I can't wait until you get here! Oh, and you won't be traveling alone. The Asimovs sent for their daughter. She'll be spacing from Luna to L-1. We have to go. Tell Grandma I'll write as soon as I can. Love you! Bye!"

One of the mobile robots rolled into the room with breakfast. "Dwarf wheat cereal. Hydro-strawberries. Orange synth-juice." When I didn't take the plate, the mobot cycled to standby. Dad was right. I never thought this day would come. But it had. I was going to Mars. So why wasn't I happy?

"At least you won't be going alone." Grandma was standing in the door-way.

"No. I get to go to Mars with a loony."

"Don't be provincial, Arcturus. Being born on Luna is pretty special. If things had been different, you'd be a 'loony' too, and you'd look down your nose at all us 'groundhogs' living in our underground apartments."

"Dad never told me the whole story . . . "

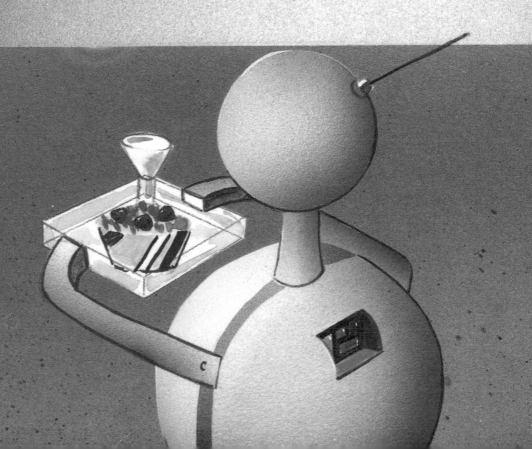

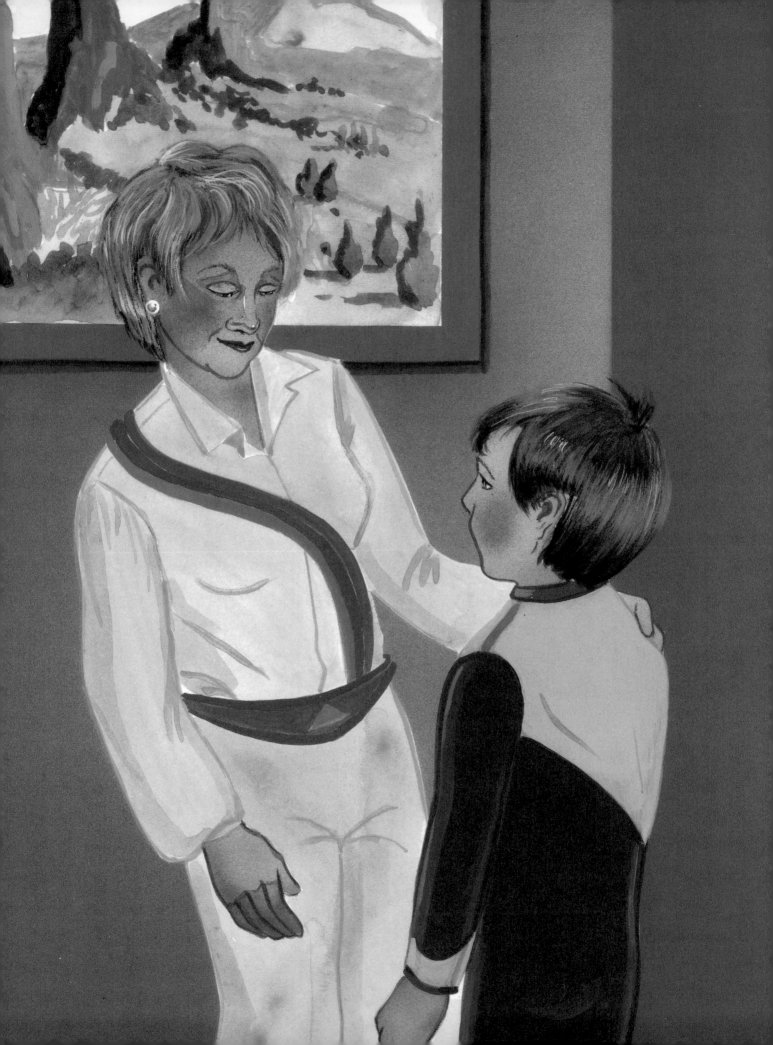

"Well, I married your grandfather Jonah in 2022 and found out I was pregnant with your father in '24. A couple of months later TRI-EMCO sent out the Tycho City job assignments. I stayed on Earth because I didn't want to be in space while I was pregnant. I was going to go after Jules was born, but then the news about Clavius reached Earth . . . "

The whole world had heard about Clavius Crater—the first, and worst, disaster in off-world mining.

"Your grandfather was one of the forty-three miners living in the base camp at the foot of the mountains. No one knows for sure what set off the avalanche—dynamite, drilling, vibrations from the heavy equipment. There's not much gravity up there, but mass is still mass, and once a boulder the size of a pyramid gets rolling . . . there wasn't much warning. Jonah was helping some other miners get into pressure suits when the biosphere was crushed. Decompression was instantaneous. The six who had their suits on survived . . . He wasn't one of them. After your father was born I went up to see the monument . . . but I could never live there.

"So, your father was raised on Earth and so were you. There must be something in our blood, though. Your father was never happy being a groundhog. He always wanted to space. For a while he flew the Orient Express for AeroStar. That wasn't enough for him so he ferried Moon ore for TerraSteel . . . that's where he met your mother. She loved space just as much as he did. TRI-EMCO built Bradbury in '60, just after you were born . . . "

I knew the rest of the story. I was eleven when Martian Mining and Manufacturing—TRI-EMCO (they're also Moon Mining and Manufacturing and Mercury Mining and Manufacturing)—advertised for a Senior Metallurgist and a Data Communications Programmer. Thousands of people applied. Since these weren't the kind of jobs you could just quit and come home if things didn't work out, TRI-EMCO figured couples would make the best employees. But it was so expensive to get them there—$500,000 each—that I had to stay Earthside with Grandma until they got enough money together.

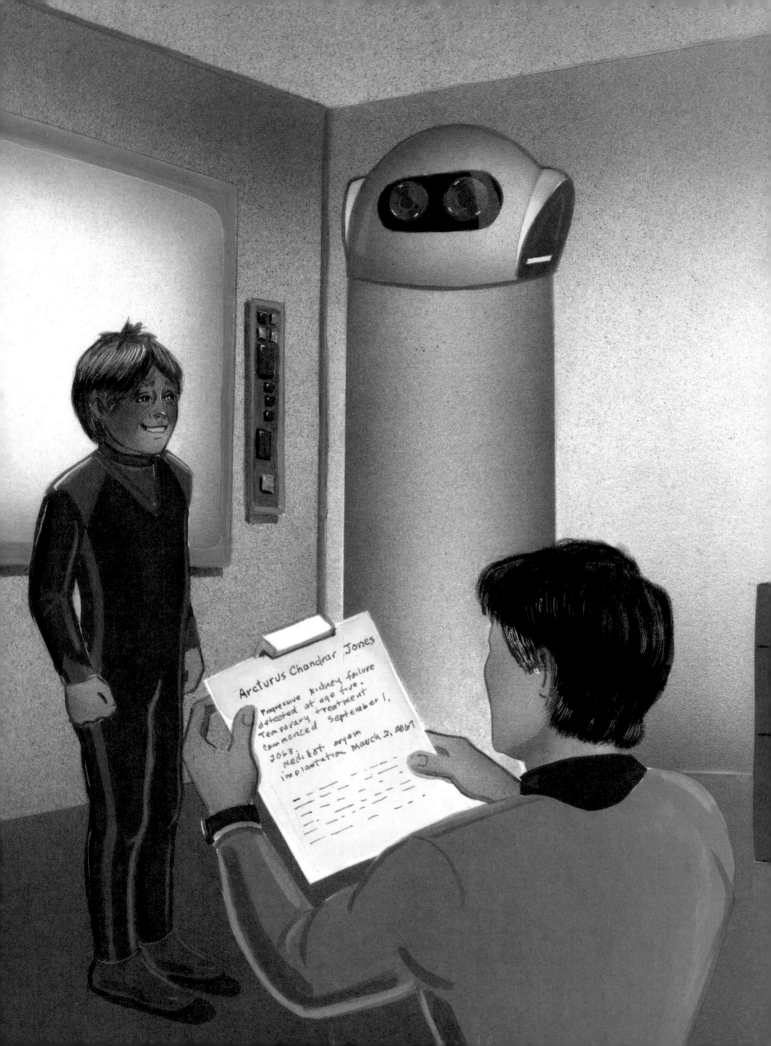

Arcturus Chandrar Jones

Progressive kidney failure
detected at age five.
Temporary treatment
commenced September 1,
3063.
Medikit organ
implantation March 2, 3067

You'd be surprised how fast those two years went by. When I wasn't busy with school or travel, I spent time studying up on things I'd need to know when they sent for me.

"They kept their promise. They sent for you."

"I know."

"So why the long face?"

"It's not like I'm moving across the street. I'll be millions of kliks away. And we both know I'll never be coming back. I'll miss you . . . and my friends."

"And we'll miss you, Arky. But those are problems pioneers always face. And don't kid yourself, that's what you'll be—a pioneer growing up on the frontier—the space frontier. A different world with new horizons and new challenges. You'll be experiencing things only a handful of others ever have. You'll be right at the edge of mankind's greatest adventure . . . "

SPACE MEDICINE

"So, you're going to Mars! Just have to make sure no unauthorized organisms try to hitch a ride with you. Don't want any diseases spread in zero-gee. When was the last time a Medibot examined you?"

"Well, I had my kidney cloned . . . "

"Ah, let's check your card." My medical history card was fastened to the top of the chart the doctor was holding. He ran it through the Medibot scanner. A synthesized voice accompanied the information on the screen:

"Patient: Arcturus Chandrar Jones. Progressive kidney failure detected at age five. Temporary treatment commenced August 3, 2063. Standard CK-201 Hopkins-Muer cell generation commenced September 1, 2063. Medibot organ-implantation March 2, 2067 . . . "

"So, you had a bad kidney and they grew you a new one. And since it was cloned from your own cells, there were no organ rejection problems . . . simple enough. Okay, in you go."

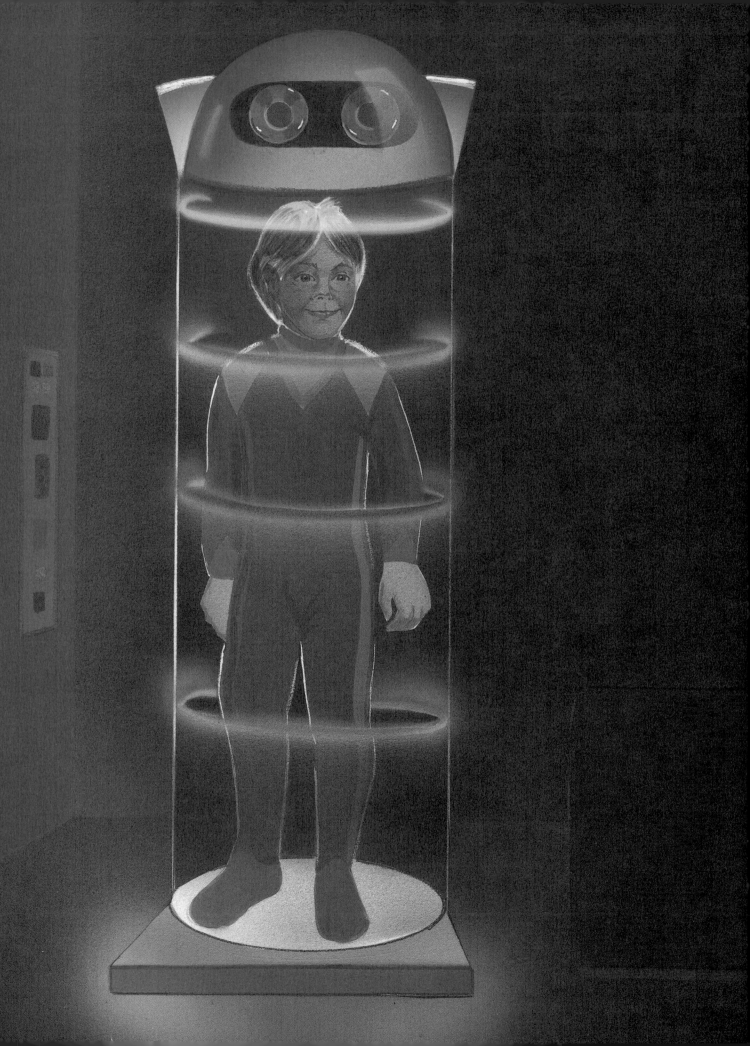

The Medibot is like a doctor's office, examination room, medical laboratory and surgery all in one. Dad says it's a "medical expert-system": It has the knowledge and experience of the best medical experts of the last two centuries stored in its computer memory. It makes a diagnosis and administers treatment just the way they would. Better, really, because it's so much faster.

I stepped inside the transparent cylinder and the lid snapped shut. The doctor's voice sounded far away.

"Head . . . eyes . . . ears . . . nose . . . throat . . . internals . . . heart . . . lungs look good . . . " All the time he talked the Medibot was scanning, probing and looking over, under, around, into and through just about every part of my body, from toes to nose—and a lot of other places. It wasn't much fun. But it didn't hurt and it only took about two minutes.

"Out you come. Any zero-gee sickness?"

"Never had it."

"You've been up before?"

"Just once to LEO-6 . . . "

"Well. Going to Mars is different from a vacation on PlayPort. You're going to be in zero- and low-gee conditions for several months. I know the ISS CLARKE is an adjustable-gravity ship, but we've treated you against calcium loss anyway. Too long in zero-gee and your bones could weaken until even Mars's light gravity would be dangerous. Your exercise program's finished printing . . . here, take this with you and use the gym on the CLARKE at least an hour a day—your heart grows weak in zero-gee too, you know. Let's see . . . what else? Oh. You'll grow about two inches taller during the trip because Earth's gravity isn't pulling down on your vertebrae anymore. You realize, of course, that after a few years on Mars your body will change so much you'll find it very difficult to return to Earth . . . "

"Grab your lifejackets and hold onto your hats! We're about to ride the wildest rapids on the Colorado River! The walls of the Grand Canyon tower over half-a-mile on either side . . . "

Living at Sub-level-18 means Grandma and I don't have any windows. But who wants to look at factories and skyways and hydroponic gardens when you can have the greatest views on Earth—live and with sound—just by pushing a button on the video frame? Every room in the house has one hanging from a wall—like picture frames, but for television. And there are cameras all over the world.

" . . . a beautiful summer day. The wind-chill factor is minus-eight degrees. Our Sherpa guide has a camera. Let's follow the expedition on the last stage of their climb up Mount Everest. Everest, at 8,848 meters, is the highest mountain on Earth. The highest mountain in the solar system is on Mars, of course . . . "

Olympus Mons is almost three times taller than Everest. Mom says she can see it through the biosphere dome. And just a few kliks southeast of Bradbury is Valles Marinaris, where the Lowell Expedition discovered the first fossils . . .

"Welcome to the Gardens of Atlantis, the newest Mid-Ocean Amusement Park, extending one klik beneath the South Pacific. Here, on man-made reefs, visitors swim with schools of bottlenose dolphins . . . "

The phone beeped, overriding the video. My history teacher's face appeared on the screen. "Arky?"

"Mr. Ikimoto. Hi."

"I hear you're moving."

"Have you told the class?"

"I didn't get the chance. They told me!"

"But I just called Pablo in Brasilia . . . "

"And he called Sienna in France . . . and she called Supatra in Sri Lanka . . . nothing travels faster than good news."

Lincoln Ikimoto teaches my World History class on LearnSat-II. All the International Education Network's satellites are in geo-synchronous orbits. That means they orbit at the same speed Earth rotates so they stay over the same location. Kids from all over the world can take classes from the best teachers in the world without leaving their houses. The only times classes meet face-to-face are for field trips. We've been to the Imperial Palace at Beijing, the Pyramid of the Sun at Teotihuacan . . .

Juan-Claude Baptiste appeared in a corner of the frame. "I hear the scuba diving on Mars is terrible, Arky."

"So send me a parrotfish from Aruba."

"Sure. As soon as you send me a fossil from Mars!"

Then Supatra Bhattacharyya popped on in another corner of the frame, "What about our holo-chess game, Arky? It's your move . . . "

"Rook to Bishop three, check. Send your next move care of the ISS CLARKE . . . "

"Arigato, Arky . . . "

"Vaya con Dios . . . "

One by one my other friends phoned in from around the world, and we said good-bye for maybe the last time.

"Du maa leve saa vel . . . "

"Sayonara, Arky-san . . . "

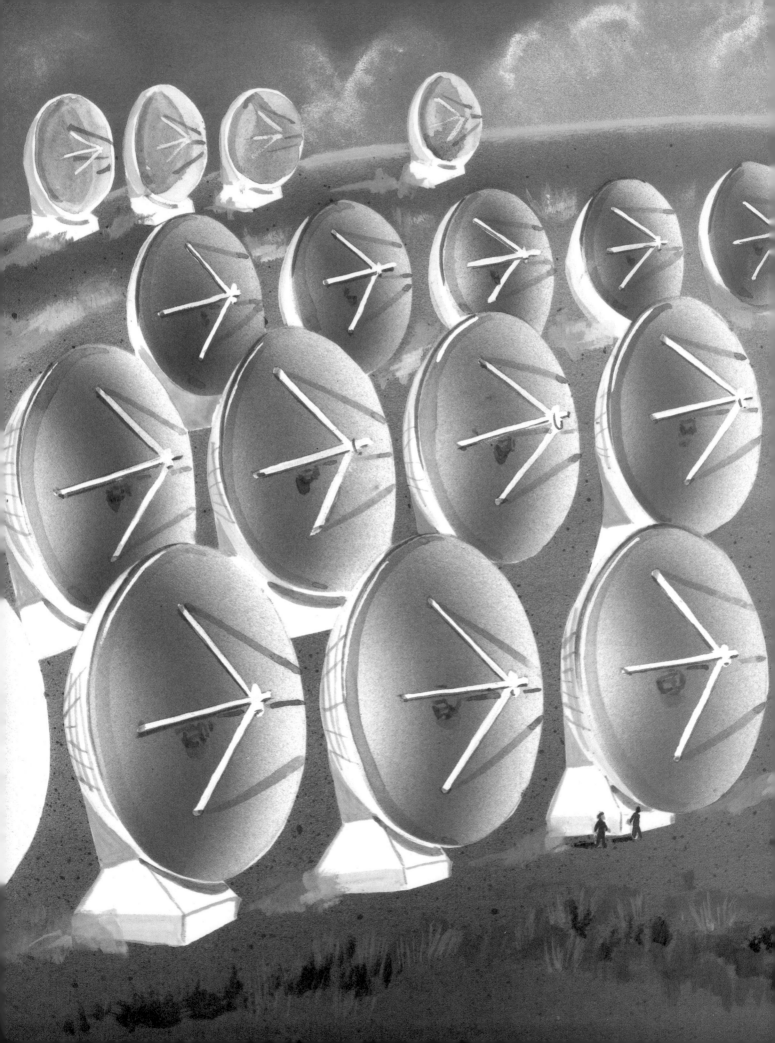

SKYWAY EXPRESS

"I've never liked these short hops, Arcturus. They're never long enough for a good nap or a movie, and all they serve is synth-juice and stale peanuts. I'll be glad when Energy Grid Systems is done with the new power grid. Maybe I'll take early retirement and come up to live with you."

"By that time you'll be the senior physicist and they'll double your salary and transfer you to the Titan platform, Grandma."

"I'm too old for off-world duty, Arky. I need a planet under my feet. Watch your step." The doors slid open and we found our seats near the front of the fuselage. I sat by the window. This would be my last trip and I didn't want to miss anything. I've always loved the desert. A good thing, I guess—Mars is all desert.

"Welcome to Skyway Express from Phoenix/Tucson Metroplex to Mojave Interplanetary Spaceport. Distance: 800 kliks. Travel time: one hour and fifteen minutes. Acceleration belts will fasten automatically." The super-conductor engines whined and soon the ground became a blur as we hit a cruising speed of 640 kliks-per-hour.

Soon the giant Gila Power Grid came into view. Grandma had helped design it—mile after mile of dish receivers automatically tracking WEST-1, one of the orbiting solar power generators. WEST-1 beams microwave energy down to the grid day and night; the grid turns it into electricity for seventy-five million people in three western states . . .

   We headed east and crossed the Castle Dome Mountains. Then north along the Colorado River to Blythe. Hundreds of hydroponic gardens flashed past, marking the roofs of underground buildings like the one we lived in. Residential buildings grow most of their own food in these huge greenhouses. Hydroponics has been around for a couple of hundred years, but didn't make it really big until the late twentieth century. Astronauts had to grow their own food during extended voyages and, since no one wanted to lift dirt into orbit, hydroponics— growing without soil— was perfect. It's how food is grown on Luna, Mars and Mercury, and on every space station and cycling spaceship in the Inner System. Plants take in carbon dioxide—what humans exhale—and give off oxygen—what humans inhale. So, in addition to food, plants are a biological air recycling system. Pretty handy!

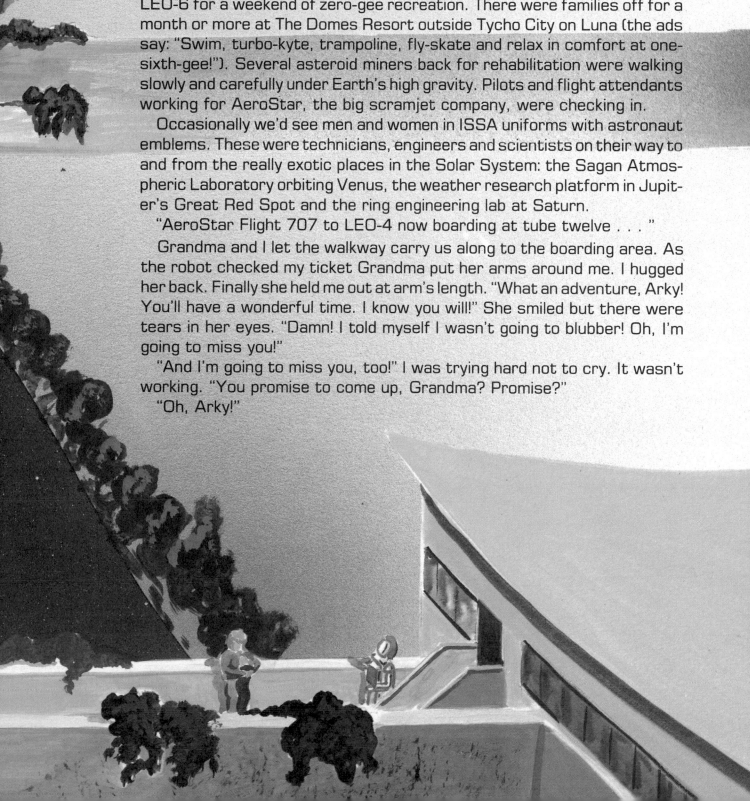

MIX

Mojave Interplanetary Spaceport is the biggest of the five spaceports. The others are Karaganda in the Central Sino-Soviet Republic, Macdonnell near Alice Springs in Australia, Nazca, Peru in the USA (Union of South America), and Sahara in the Northern African States: MIX, KIX, MAX, NIX and SIX.

The crowd and the noise were incredible. MIX is run by ISSA of course, but at least half the traffic is commercial. We saw tourists on their way to LEO-6 for a weekend of zero-gee recreation. There were families off for a month or more at The Domes Resort outside Tycho City on Luna (the ads say: "Swim, turbo-kyte, trampoline, fly-skate and relax in comfort at one-sixth-gee!"). Several asteroid miners back for rehabilitation were walking slowly and carefully under Earth's high gravity. Pilots and flight attendants working for AeroStar, the big scramjet company, were checking in.

Occasionally we'd see men and women in ISSA uniforms with astronaut emblems. These were technicians, engineers and scientists on their way to and from the really exotic places in the Solar System: the Sagan Atmospheric Laboratory orbiting Venus, the weather research platform in Jupiter's Great Red Spot and the ring engineering lab at Saturn.

"AeroStar Flight 707 to LEO-4 now boarding at tube twelve . . . "

Grandma and I let the walkway carry us along to the boarding area. As the robot checked my ticket Grandma put her arms around me. I hugged her back. Finally she held me out at arm's length. "What an adventure, Arky! You'll have a wonderful time. I know you will!" She smiled but there were tears in her eyes. "Damn! I told myself I wasn't going to blubber! Oh, I'm going to miss you!"

"And I'm going to miss you, too!" I was trying hard not to cry. It wasn't working. "You promise to come up, Grandma? Promise?"

"Oh, Arky!"

GOOD-BYE EARTH

"Launch crew, clear the apron and staging areas. Stand by for runway clearance."

"On-board power engaged."

"Clearance on runway 55-B. AeroStar 707, on my mark, you are ten minutes from takeoff. Mark."

"Flight computer standing by."

"This is Flight Manager Diana Rumonov. Welcome aboard AeroStar Flight 707 bound for Space Station LEO-4. Our single-stage, liquid-hydrogen fueled, supersonic combustion scramjet has a top speed of Mach-22, or approximately twenty-five thousand kliks-per-hour . . . "

"On my mark switching ground launch sequencer to on-board computer. Mark."

"Flight computer engaged. Launch sequencer programmed."

"We'll reach low Earth orbit and begin docking procedures at LEO-4 after a flight time of approximately twenty minutes . . . "

"Tanks pressurized."

"All hydraulics go."

"Make sure all carry-on luggage is stored. And, if you experience zero-gee sickness, please use the receptacle on the back of the chair in front of you. We don't want any loose matter floating around the cabin . . . "

"Taxi runway 55-B."

"In case of orbital emergency, each chair is equipped with an automatic pressure bag that unfolds to cover your entire body. A flight attendant will demonstrate. Each bag contains emergency water and air supplies for up to twenty-four hours. A rescue team can reach us in less than half an hour . . . "

"AeroStar 707 you are sixty seconds from takeoff. Begin automatic countdown."

"Launch sequencer engaged."

"Flight attendants, prepare for takeoff."

The roar of the engines began to build, like thunder from a distant storm. We rolled down the runway, picking up speed.

"Main engines are go."

Moments later, riding the fire of millions of horsepower, I left Earth for the last time.

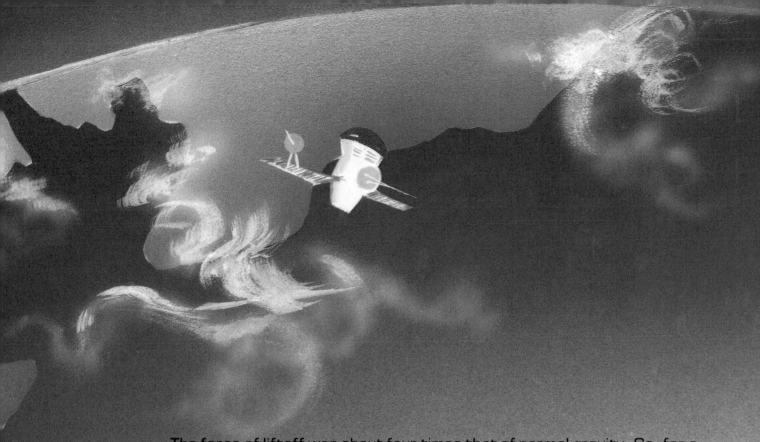

The force of liftoff was about four times that of normal gravity. So, for a few minutes, I weighed over one thousand kilos! It felt like a tag team of sumo wrestlers was sitting on my chest.

"This is your Flight Manager. We have completed orbital insertion and are currently 410 kliks above the equator, orbiting west-to-east."

I took a deep breath as the wrestlers got off. Phew! As I relaxed, my arm floated off the armrest by itself; across the aisle a woman's hair was standing straight up on end, waving like grass in the wind. Of course! We were in orbit—we were weightless!

"As we prepare for docking, we will be rotating our craft one hundred and eighty degrees, giving you a clear view of Earth through the overhead windows."

I know you've seen pictures of the Earth from space, but nothing compares to the real thing. It was dawn over Eastern Africa. I could see the Serengeti Plains. And the snow on Mount Kilimanjaro glittered like jewelry in the sun. As we drifted over India and Sri Lanka I wondered what Supatra was doing. Strange to think that up here, orbiting at 27,000 kliks-per-hour, sunrise happens every hour and a half . . .

"Mommy, I have to go!"

"Davey, I told you to go before we left!"

"I forgot."

I watched as the attendant, wearing Velcro® space sandals, towed the kid behind her like a kite on a string. I remembered learning how to use the bathroom in zero-gee conditions. I hoped the kid had a change of clothing handy . . .

"If you're interested in a brief audio tour of some of the things you'll be seeing, plug your earphone into the comm console in front of you." I was, and did.

"Since the middle of the last century, nations have been launching satellites and building stations in space. There are currently over fifteen hundred satellites in low Earth orbit. They are used by government and private industry for communications, weather forecasting, crop analysis, oil and mineral prospecting and monitoring the environment.

"There are eight space stations in equatorial and polar orbits. Among them are LEO-1, the micro-gravity research station, LEO-2 and -3, operated by IPT&T for Earth and long-range communications, and LEO-4, the primary transfer station for travelers to Luna and L-1. The Hubble Telescope—the first space-based telescope—is in orbit several hundred kliks ahead of us.

"Further out, 35,000 kliks from Earth, are many special factories for the manufacture of pure crystals, chemicals and special drugs that can only be made in the complete vacuum, zero-gravity conditions found in space. Here also are the giant power stations, such as WEST-1 and the LearnSats, run by the International Education Network.

"Finally, 350,000 kliks from Earth, is L-1, jumping off point to the solar system . . . "

Slowly, gracefully, LEO-4 drifted into view: a frozen labyrinth of delicate girders, struts and beams connecting modules of all different sizes and shapes. There were fuel storage modules, hydroponic modules, work areas, living areas . . .

Remote arms operated from a control center inside the station reached out and latched onto our plane, gently pulling us into the docking module. There was a dull "clang" as the two airlocks sealed, and a faint hiss as the pressure equalized.

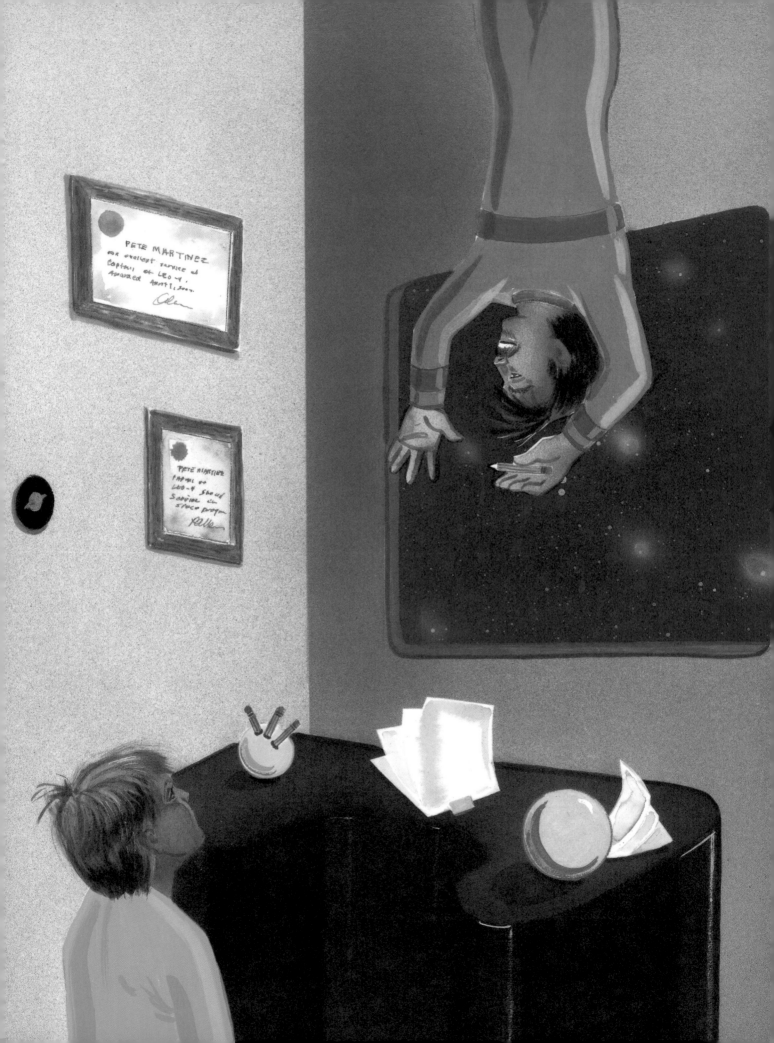

LEO-4

"Passenger Arcturus Jones?"

"Are you kidding?"

"Passenger Arcturus Jones?"

"Don't be silly."

"Passenger Arcturus Jones?"

"Yes, that's me."

"Please accompany me to the General Manager's office." I followed the mobot through the waiting room, my sandals sticking and unsticking to Velcro® strips on the floor. Once you get used to weightlessness it's easier, faster and a lot more fun to just push off of the nearest surface and glide, but I wasn't ready for that yet.

I pushed my luggage through the air ahead of me down a long corridor. The General Manager's office was in the Administration Module. The door opened automatically and I went in. I looked around, but didn't see anybody.

"Jones?"

"Oh! Uh, yes, sir." He was floating behind his desk directly overhead. Of course, in zero-gee, words such as "over," "under," "up" and "down" don't really have any meaning. But talking to someone whose face is upside down, relative to yours, and whose feet are on the "ceiling" still takes some getting used to.

"Welcome to LEO-4. I'm Pete Martinez. They tell me I run this place. But, between you and me, all I really do is shuffle papers and snarl at the mobots. Take off those sandals and push yourself up here so I can see what J.V.'s kid looks like right-side up."

"You know my dad?"

"Jules Verne Jones and I ferried rocks for TerraSteel a couple of years before you were born—before he met your mother and went back dirtside to get his degrees. We keep in touch. He called yesterday to tell me you'd be up. Said I should keep an eye on you or you'd be running this place before long . . . You're not after my job are you?"

I liked him. "Uh, no, sir. Not yet anyway." I grinned.

"Good. Like the view?" I learned later that the giant window behind his desk was the largest on the station. It looked out past the antennae and power grids to Earth; to its green hills, blue oceans and white clouds. I felt a lump in my throat and a stinging in my eyes.

"It's . . . it's . . . "

"Yeah, it sure is. Exactly the way I feel about it too. But space is just as beautiful—in a different way. And, from everything I hear, they're turning Mars into a paradise. Wish I was going with you. Your transfer vehicle isn't due until tomorrow morning. How would you like to visit TerraSteel and watch them shovel some coal?"

"Freighter, 500 meters and closing. Speed, two kliks."

"Locking sequencer programmed."

"Initiate locking sequence."

"OMV in position . . . and . . . locking."

"Firing sequence one programmed."

"Clear the firing area."

"All clear."

Shining in the black vacuum of space in front of us was the largest off-world factory in the Solar System; 400 kliks below was the crescent Earth with lights from a few big cities sparkling here and there; 300,000 kliks above was the full moon. What a sight! I was thankful for the straps and the safety lines hooked to my suit and our two-man space scooter.

"Control, we have visitors out here."

"That you, Pete?"

"Affirmative, Annie. And say hi to Arky Jones."

"J.V. and Octavia's boy?"

"The very same. Arky, say hello to 'Tugboat Annie' Bowes, scourge of the spaceways and the best tug pilot in the system."

"You know Mom and Dad too?"

"I introduced your mother to J.V. Now *there* was some kind of pilot. He could handle anything from a tug to a scramjet . . . "

"Firing sequence two programmed."

"Hold on. Let me nudge this barge. Clear the firing area."

"All clear."

The "barge" was a robot freighter longer than any ten city blocks. It was filled with high-grade ore from Luna. The "tug" was a remote-controlled Orbital Maneuvering Vehicle used to launch satellites and maneuver manned and unmanned transfer vehicles and freighters. Annie was operating the OMV from inside the TerraSteel platform by watching video monitors and listening to the space-suited docking team outside. The jets fired again and the freighter moved slowly toward the loading dock.

"When they finish unloading, the ore will be turned into ultrasteel through a process that can only be used in zero-gee conditions. The molten metal is injected with billions of gas bubbles, making it super light, while keeping it as strong as conventional steel. All the new space stations are built with ultrasteel, as well as most big new buildings on Earth . . . "

"Bring Arky aboard, Pete."

"No time this trip, Annie. We've got to get back so he can catch a lift out to L-1."

"Maybe next time then. Arky, say hi to your Mom and Dad. You're gonna love Mars."

"I hope so. Pete, can I drive back?"

"Think you know how?"

"Sure. Hang on."

The MMU—Manned Maneuvering Unit, or "space scooter," used compressed nitrogen gas, jetted through nozzles, to move through space. I pushed the controls. "Whoa! What did I do wrong?!" We were tumbling tail over tea kettle (that's how Grandma would describe it), completely out of control.

Tugboat Annie came on the comm line, "Hey, Pete! Are you sure that's J.V.'s kid?" It took a long time for the crew to stop laughing. It took even longer for me to get the scooter back under control. Pete insisted I do it myself. Finally I did, and we headed back.

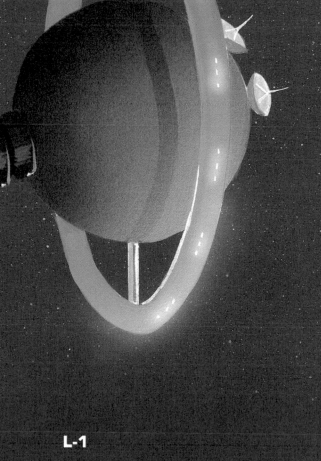

L-1

"TV-12 this is L-1, OMV control, preparing for lockup and docking."

There are five libration points in the Earth-Moon system (sometimes called Lagrange points, after the French mathematician who calculated their existence). These are points in space where objects have very stable orbits. Libration point one—L-1—is between the Earth and the Moon, 350,000 kliks from Earth.

The transfer vehicle was a little cramped, but the trip had only taken a couple of days, so it wasn't too bad. There were eight of us aboard; two were heading to L-1 to start new jobs, three scientists would continue to the ring station at Saturn, and two "skydivers"—space construction workers—heading for L-5 where O'NEILL was under construction. When it was done, O'NEILL would be a giant orbiting home in space for almost a million people.

"This is TV-12. Roger, L-1, we have the tug in view. Initiating OMV locking sequence . . . now. We're all yours."

I was standing by a small observation window when the OMV turned us toward L-1. "Wow."

"Really something, isn't it?" One of the ring engineers had come up beside me.

"It's huge."

"Has to be. It's a hotel, garage, rescue base, construction center, research station, launching platform . . . " The series of inter-connected spheres stretched out for almost a klik. Several were circled by huge wheels. "Those are the gravity-normal sections . . . for living quarters, restaurants, hydroponic gardens . . . "

LOONY AND THE GROUNDHOG

The waiting room was as big as a hotel lobby—and more crowded. I looked around and finally saw an information booth on the ceiling about twenty meters away. Since the shortest way was through the air, I decided to try out my "space legs." I took off my sandals and gave a push. Hey, this zero-gee stuff was fun!

When I pushed off I forgot to look and see if anyone was coming.

"Ooof. Watch it!"

"Hey! Steer clear!"

"Sorry. Uh, oh." By the time I realized I was in trouble, it was too late. I was in the middle of a thrashing, confused ball of people stuck in the air in the middle of the waiting room.

"There goes my suitcase!"

"Someone grab my dog!"

People, suitcases, briefcases, a cane, and a small, confused dog drifted around. In zero-gee, without a fixed surface to push off from, it was going to be difficult for any of us to get anywhere.

"Everybody! Stop yelling! Stop moving! We can get things back to normal if you'll just calm down and listen!" She was about my age and height. But thinner, with dark hair done up in braids. The only other thing I had time to notice was that she was as angry as a wet cat. "You! Yes, you. The groundhog who started this mess! Don't you know the Newton Maneuver? Well then who let you up here without a nursemaid? Never mind. You with the dog. Take that lady's hand . . . pull yourselves past each other and let go . . . right . . . now!" As soon as they let go they flew in opposite directions, one toward one end of the waiting room, one toward the other. Of course! How simple!

"'For every action there is an opposite and equal reaction.' Isaac Newton's Third Law of Motion. Remember it. Now, the rest of you pair up. And watch where you're going. Especially you, Groundhog . . . "

When I finally got to my room there was a message telling me to report to the General Manager's office in the Admin Module. As I walked in she was talking on the intercom, "And get a crew down to finish cleaning up the waiting room . . . I don't care what Ambassador Amarado says. He knows better than to bring a dog up that isn't space-trained . . . .What a mess! Ah. Come in, come in. You must be Arcturus Jones. I'd like you to meet Ilena Asimov . . . " I hadn't noticed the other person in the office. "Ilena just got here from Luna. You'll be traveling to Mars together . . . "

I recognized the hairstyle before she even turned around. "You?!"

"Oh, no. The Groundhog!"

ISS CLARKE

Captain was talking, "It's a simple concept, really. Think of cycling spaceships as ocean liners that continuously sail from Earth to Mars and back to Earth. We'll match orbits, park the transfer vehicle in the garage, and spend about five months on board the ISS CLARKE. Then, when we reach Mars, we'll pile back into the TV and head down to Bradbury. The ISS CLARKE never stops. As we leave, passengers from Mars get aboard and head back to the Earth-Moon system."

"But why do it that way?"

"Because speed is expensive, Groundhog. It takes lots of reactor mass to boost a payload into orbit. With cycling spaceships, you only have to accelerate once . . . "

"Hey, Loony, I wouldn't call someone a 'groundhog' if I couldn't even carry my own suitcase." She might be able to fly like a bird in zero-gee, but, in the Earth-normal sections of L-1, Ilena Asimov was as weak as a baby. I almost felt sorry for her. Almost.

"A little exercise and I won't need anyone's help . . . "

"If you two can't get along any better than this, I'll let everyone vote to see if we should use both of you for reactor mass. In fact . . . "

We were saved by the bell. The intercom bell, that is. "The seatbelt sign is lit. Firing sequences now being programmed. The Captain will please report to the flight deck."

Even from a distance the ISS CLARKE was awesome: two giant spheres at either end of a two-klik-long shaft; another thicker section, about half-a-klik long, ran perpendicular to that, bisecting it and acting as an axis of rotation for the whole structure. It was spinning like a ballet dancer, about one revolution-per-minute, which supplied artificial gravity to the spheres. The center section, of course, remained in zero-gee.

"Those shafts are elevators that take you from one sphere to the other . . . "

"I know, Loony. And that center module is where the garage, engines and research labs are."

"Look! The spheres are moving up the elevator shafts! They're slowing the ship's spin."

I grinned at her. "That's Newton's Principle of Conservation of Momentum. It's like a skater spinning on ice pulling his arms in . . . the closer his arms are to his body—his axis of rotation—the faster he spins . . . "

"And the further out his arms are, the slower he spins. I knew that . . . Groundhog."

It was going to be a long trip.

SPACE MAIL TRANSMISSION MAY 2, 2071.
FROM: A.C. Jones, ISS CLARKE, Earth-to-Mars transit.
TO: Bellavia M. Charming-Jones, 94582-A, Sub-level 18, Phoenix/
Tucson Metroplex, United North America, Earth. Recording.

"Grandma. I'm taping this while I'm working at my new job—assistant hydroponist. The last time I wrote, I was working in food preparation, but that was before I spilled orange synth-juice in the zero-gee cafeteria. You should have seen Captain's face when he looked up and saw that big glob of juice floating toward him. It's a good thing his mouth was open or it all would have gone to waste . . .

"The hydroponics module is under spin gravity equal to Mars's surface. Plants have to have some kind of gravity or their roots don't know which way to grow. There must be two acres of plants here. Potatoes, carrots, peas, beans, lettuce, some dwarf orange and lemon trees. You name it and we grow it—flowers too. It smells just like home. And the food's great. Not just the fresh vegetables and fruit, but steak, seafood, puddings . . ."

"Feed me. Feed me, Arky."

"Sorry. That's the Captain's idea of a joke. A taped reminder for me to check the fertilizer level. All waste products get recycled for fertilizer, just like air and water waste. But the robots do all the important jobs. I get to do the smelly ones. Be right back . . ."

"Hey, Arky! Come up to the observation deck! You gotta see this."

"Be right there! That's Loony on the intercom. Uh, I mean, Ilena Asimov. We're the only kids on the ship so I try to get along with her. Captain's orders. Actually, she's not too bad . . ."

"Groundhog! Come on!"

"I'll finish this later . . ."

FEAR AND PANIC

"Look," Ilena said, "Phobos and Deimos. Uh, that means 'fear' and 'panic' in Latin." A huge projection of Mars filled the viewscreen on the observation deck. Its two tiny moons were dark dots against the planet's red surface. Phobos, the largest of the two, was almost beyond the horizon.

"Since Mars was named for the Roman god of war, I guess astronomers thought his two servants ought to have warlike names."

"John Carter called them the 'hurtling moons of Barsoom.'"

"Who did what?" I asked.

"In the beginning of the twentieth century, when people still thought Mars was inhabited, Edgar Rice Burroughs wrote *A Princess of Mars*. His hero was named John Carter. He had all kinds of wild adventures on Barsoom—that's what he said the Martians called their planet. And when he watched Phobos and Deimos racing through the night sky, that's how he described them."

"Well, with Phobos orbiting once every seven and a half hours, and Deimos once every thirty hours, I guess they would look like they were hurtling. Hey! Look at that flame! I'll bet that's from the propellant factory." A thin line of fire appeared near the surface of Phobos where TRI-EMCO operated a refueling plant. "I wonder what Mr. Burroughs would have thought if he had known the moons of Barsoom were going to supply the fuel we need to reach the rest of the solar system . . . . "

"Hey! How about some skating? Beat you to the rink!"

"Wait up! Ow!" I still couldn't fly very well . . . I pushed myself into the side of a door.

FUN AND GAMES

Fly-skating is one sport that'll never catch on back home—too much gravity—but in space, it's perfect. If you like roller-skating at seventy-five kliks-an-hour . . .

The rink was a fifteen-meter sphere at one end of the low-gee section of the ship. Half a dozen other passengers were skating too. It's great exercise. Someone with Earth muscles, like me, gets a chance to build up speed and maintain it for maybe an hour, pumping the legs, working up a sweat, getting the heart going. Just what the Medibot ordered.

"Hey, Groundhog! Watch this!" Lena passed me like I was standing still. She must have been doing fifty. She's used to low gravity, so to her fly-skating is practically an Olympic event. It combines speed, endurance, dancing and diving.

"Go for it!" I yelled. She pulled her arms back and crouched low, like a diver about to enter the water. With a burst, she uncoiled all that energy, pushing herself off the floor of the rink in a furious, tumbling dive. An instant later she landed skate-first against the opposite wall and propelled herself into a dizzying spin which she gradually slowed. She finished with a series of complex turns and spins in tuck, layout and pike positions before landing feather-soft against the far wall. She was breathing heavily and grinning.

Everyone in the room burst into wild applause. On a scale of one to ten I gave her . . . a twelve.

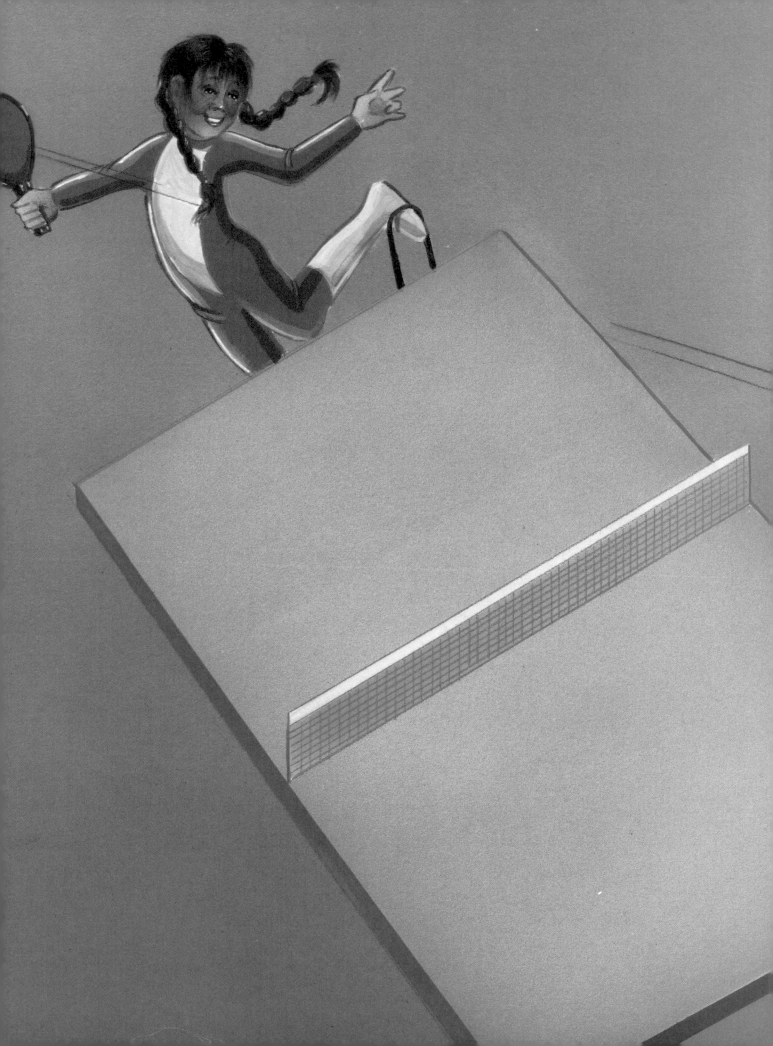

"Hey, got any energy left over for some Ping-Pong®?"

"Only if you play with both hands tied behind your back and your eyes shut."

"Come on. I'll spot you eight points."

"Well, all right."

We hooked our feet into the elastic straps that pull you back when you lunge to hit a ball. "Your serve!"

With a few minor adjustments, Ping-Pong® in space is pretty much the same as on Earth . . . fast, furious and fun. We talked in between points.

"How was it you were raised on the Moon?"

"I was born there. Second generation, actually. Ugh! Nice shot."

"So your folks were born there too?"

"My grandfather was in the first crew that went up to Clavius in '24."

"In '24? Then your grandfather . . . "

"Yeah. He was one of the survivors . . . said the only reason he made it was that another miner helped him with his pressure suit just before the biosphere was crushed. Grandpa called him a hero . . . Hey! Groundhog! How could you miss that shot?"

MARSFALL

"You have the helm, Captain. Have a safe trip."

"Thank you, Captain. Have a good stay on Mars. Over and out."

"Flight Officer Smith."

"Captain?"

"Take her down."

"Disengaging in five . . . four . . . three . . . two . . . one. Disengage."

"Firing sequence programmed."

"Initiate firing sequence."

As we slowly fell away from the huge spaceship toward the waiting planet below, the "hurtling moons of Barsoom" tumbled into view. Mars itself was shrouded in darkness. All I could see was the horizon—brilliant red, as though burning with distant fires—and a wisp of cloud trailing from the top of an ancient volcano.

"Arky, look! South of the volcano! There's Bradbury."

City lights twinkled like distant stars. My parents were waiting for me down there. Along with a new life . . . new friends . . . new adventures. Hello, Mars.

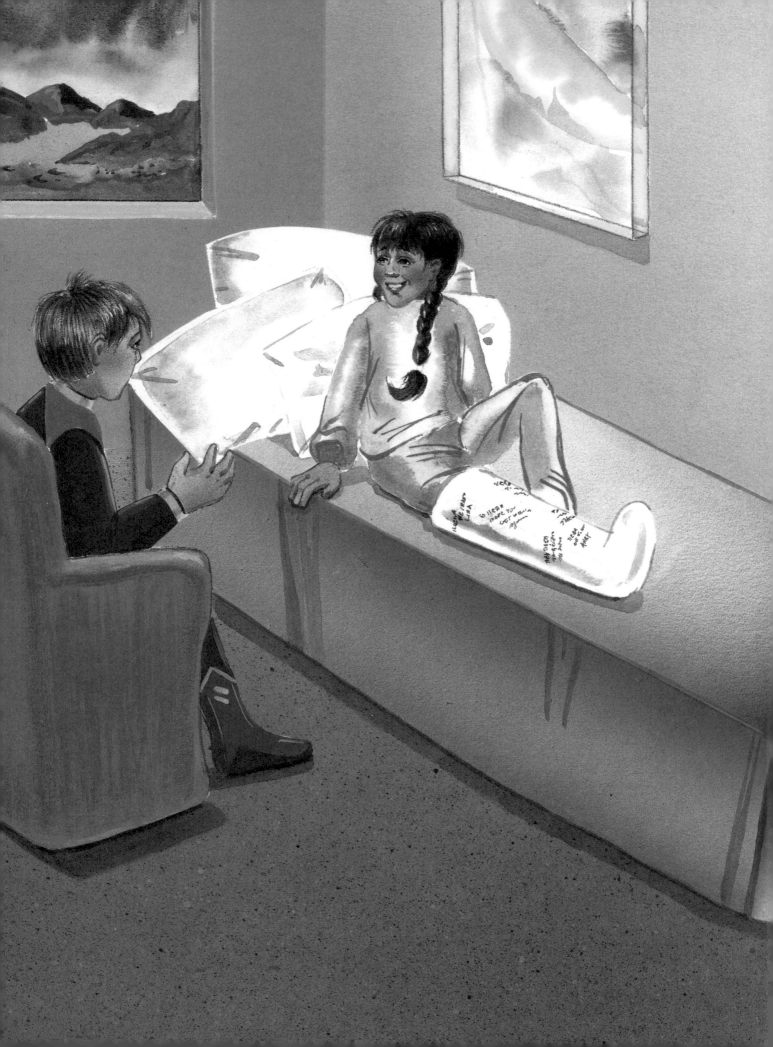

SPACE MAIL TRANSMISSION AUGUST 14, 2071.
FROM: A.C. Jones, drop-box 12-B, Bradbury, Mars.
TO: Bellavia M. Charming-Jones, 94582-A, Sub-level 18, Phoenix/Tucson
Metroplex, United North America, Earth. Recording.

"Grandma. We were almost goners. The dust storm missed us. But Dad
was so worried he forgot to be upset. Mom was almost in tears. I'm in the
doghouse. Actually, I'm in the hospital. No, no. I'm okay. I'm visiting Ilena.
She broke her leg. She must have slid three or four hundred meters down
the side of the canyon. It's lucky only the first layer of her pressure suit was
torn, and that the dust storm missed us."

"Hey! Tell her how it feels to be a hero."

"Ah, come on . . . that's Loony again. She keeps telling people . . . "

"How a groundhog climbed down the side of that cliff and brought me
back up before my air ran out."

"P.S. I told you EGS would make you Senior Physicist. And since you need
a planet under your feet, we're glad it's going to be Mars. See you soon.
Love, Arky."

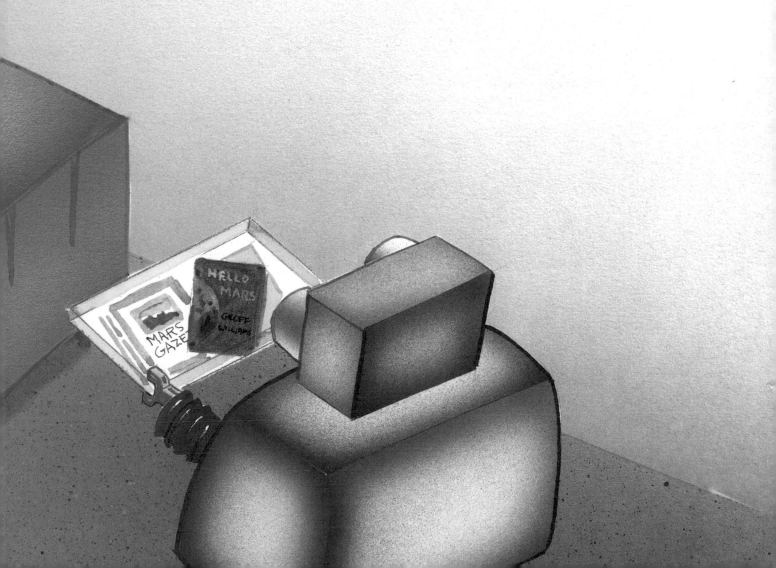

HIGHLIGHTS IN SPACE

TWENTIETH CENTURY

Date	Country/Agency	Name	Mission
10/04/57	USSR	Sputnik	Launch of first satellite
07/15/65	USA	Mariner	Flyby of Mars
07/20/69	USA	Apollo-10	Manned lunar landing
11/27/71	USSR	Mars 2	Mars orbiter/lander
1971	USSR	Salyut-1	Earth-orbiting space station
07/20/76	USA	Viking 1	Mars orbiter/lander
1989	USSR	Mars B	Landing/unmanned scientific station on Phobos
09/13/92	USA	Observer	Mars orbiter
10/03/96	USSR/USA	Glasnost-1	Mars sample/return
02/18/96	USA/ESA	Cassini-Titan	Probe of Saturn's moon Titan
09/14/98	USA	Freedom	Low Earth orbit space station

TWENTY-FIRST CENTURY

Date	Country/Agency	Name	Mission
12/01/03	USA/USSR	Fellowship-1	Humans land on Mars
07/17/01	USA	Luna	Humans set up lunar outpost
11/02/05	LOCKHEED/MITSUBISHI	Starliner	Mach 25 scramjet spaceplane
09/06/11	USA/USSR	LFRO	Lunar Farside Radio Observatory
04/04/12		Glasnost-3	First humans set up Martian outpost
04/01/17	USA/ESA/USSR/PASA	L-1	Lagrange 1 Spaceport
03/30/19	Tri-Enco	Tycho City	Lunar mining operations/mass driver
01/20/20		Delos	Lunar Orbital Processing Plant #1
11/04/21	ISSA	M-2-S	Mars Space Station established on Phobos
04/12/23	ISSA/LOCKHEED/MITSUBISHI	ISS Clarke	First Earth-Mars cycling spaceship
09/06/36	ISSA	Olympus	Base 107°W, 5°N fully operated by humans
11/17/31	Tri-Enco	Hades	Mercury Polar Mining Base
05/21/40		P-3	Phobos Propellent Plant
02/18/44		Astrid	Asteroid belt mining operations
07/04/50	ISSA-L-5	O'Neill	Lagrange-5 City in Space
10/11/60	Tri-Enco	Bradbury	Mining/Communications 128°W 20°N
02/12/66	ISSA	ISS Hawking	Construction begun on nuclear powered interstellar "seed" ship at L-1

ESA — European Space Agency
PASA — Pan Asian Space Agency
ISSA — Inner System Space Agency

2019, ISSA is a group of Space-faring countries including United North America, United South America, Sino-Soviet Union, Pan-Asian Nations, Indo-Australia and the Euro Federation, who joined together for the peaceful exploration of the solar system.